The Lion and The Mouse

AND OTHER AESOP'S FABLES

The Lion and The Mouse

AND OTHER AESOP'S FABLES

Retold by **Doris Orgel** ✒ *Illustrated by* **Bert Kitchen**

Dorling Kindersley Publishing, Inc.

For Julian
—D.O.
To Muriel, Corinna, and Saskia
—B.K.

Ink

Dorling Kindersley Publishing, Inc.
95 Madison Avenue
New York, New York 10016

Text copyright © 2000 by Doris Orgel
Illustrations copyright © 2000 by Bert Kitchen

A catalog record for this book is available from the Library of Congress.

ISBN 0-7894-2665-X

Color reproduction by Dot Gradations, UK
Printed and bound in Hong Kong by L.Rex

First American Edition, 2000

Published simultaneously in Great Britain by Dorling Kindersley Limited.

2 4 6 8 10 9 7 5 3 1

The illustrations for this book were created with watercolor and gouache.

The publisher would like to thank the following for their kind permission
to reproduce their photographs: c= centre; b= bottom; l= left; r= right; t= top
AKG London: Erich Lessing 20br, 30tr; **E.T. Archive:** 7tl, 13cra, 23tr, 28br;
Mary Evans Picture Library: 6c, 9cra, 11cra, 14br, 25br;
Spectrum Colour Library: D&J Heaton 27c.

see our complete
catalog at
www.dk.com

Contents

Introduction

(In this introduction, you, the reader, ask the questions. I, as reteller, try to give answers.)

Who Was Aesop?

Aesop was a slave, and later was set free. He lived in ancient Greece approximately two thousand six hundred years ago. And he told the kind of stories that are known as "Aesop's fables."

What are the fables about?

They are usually about animals who talk and act a lot like humans.

But in real life animals can't talk, and they don't act like humans. So the fables aren't true, are they?

They are made up, but they mean something true. For instance, in *The Lion and the Mouse*, the story shows that someone very small can sometimes help in a big way. *That's* something true.

How many Aesop's fables are there?

No one knows exactly. Many thousands.

How could Aesop have written them all?

He couldn't. Writing was still new back then, and slaves didn't go to school. It's quite likely Aesop never learned to write at all. He told his fables, and the people Aesop told his fables to passed them on, and made up fables of their own. You can, too.

Why are Aesop's fables still around after two thousand six hundred years?

I think it is because Aesop's fables are surprising, wonderfully short, and fun. Moreover, what they mean is just as wise and true today as it was way back then.

What do you think? Wait, don't answer yet. First, read the fables in this book.

Doris Orgel

The Lion *and* The Mouse

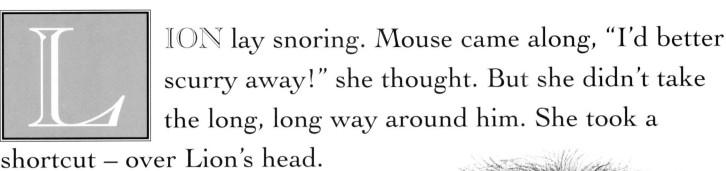

LION lay snoring. Mouse came along, "I'd better scurry away!" she thought. But she didn't take the long, long way around him. She took a shortcut – over Lion's head.

"Who's tickling my nose?" he roared and grabbed her by the tail.

"Don't eat me up," Mouse begged.

"Why not?" Lion roared even louder.

"Because I promise I'll pay you back someday," Mouse cried.

Lion laughed aloud, but let her go.

Some days later, hunters caught Lion and they tied him up.

Mouse heard him roaring. She came running, started
gnawing at the rope, and gnawed and gnawed until it frazzled.

"There, I've set you free," she squeaked, and scampered off.

*Aesop lived in ancient
Greece in the 6th
century BC. His real
name was Aisopos
(I-SOP-POSS). Here
it is spelled in Latin.*

The Mice *and* The Cat

THE mice were holding a meeting. It was about the cat. "How can we protect ourselves?" they asked. "We need a warning that he's near."

Many mice gave their ideas. "I know, I know," one mouse exclaimed: "Let's tie a bell around his neck. That way, when we hear it tinkle, we'll have time to run and hide in the nearest hole."

"Yes, yes," squeaked all the mice. And everyone agreed this was the best idea.

"Very well," said Madam Chairmouse, "who'll volunteer to put the bell on the cat?"

How many mice, do you suppose, came forward?

Not one!

In Aesop's time, cats were popular pets. They were also useful for ridding homes of mice and rats.

The Frogs, King Log, and King Crane

 E'RE tired of ruling ourselves," croaked the frogs, and asked Zeus for a king.

Zeus threw down a log to the frogs.

Fearing what this king might do, the frogs hid in the mud.

King Log kept very still.

Nervously they climbed on him. He did not protest, and even let them dive off him and sun themselves on him.

The frogs grew bored with this motionless king and croaked, "We want a livelier one!"

So Zeus sent them down a crane.

King Crane stalked around on his long, quick legs. *Snap, snap, gulp, gulp* — soon just one frog remained.

"If only we'd left well enough alone!" was the one remaining frog's last wish. Then he, too, disappeared into lively King Crane's gullet.

In the ancient Greeks' religion, Zeus lived in a palace on top of Mount Olympus. He was king of all the gods and goddesses, and of humans down on earth.

The Fox *and* The Goat

OX fell into a deep well and couldn't get out.

Sometime later Goat came by. "Is the well water good to drink?" he inquired.

"Excellent," Fox answered. "Jump in. Taste it for yourself."

Goat jumped in and drank his fill. "Now, how do we get out?" he asked.

"That's not so easy," Fox replied. "But I have a plan: Raise your front legs high up against the side of the well."

Goat did.

Fox jumped on Goat's back, climbed up, and prepared to leap out of the well.

"But how will *I* get out?" asked Goat.

"I'll grab your front legs and pull," Fox promised, leaping over Goat's head and out.

"I'm ready. Pull my legs!" Goat called. "You promised!"

But Fox had crossed the field by then, and vanished into the woods.

It's known that Aesop was a slave. Slavery was widespread in his time, and often wars were fought for the purpose of enslaving defeated enemies.

The Jackdaw

BIRDS preparing for a beauty contest were bathing in a pool. They primped, and fluffed their feathers.

A jackdaw arrived as they flew off. "How fine they look!" he sighed. "Oh, why am I so plain?"

Just then some brightly colored feathers that the birds had dropped came floating by.

He quickly fished them out and put them on. "Now I look fine," he cawed, and off he flew.

"Splendid!" said the contest judge, admiring the jackdaw. He was about to give him the prize when…

"That's mine," twittered a swallow, plucking a feather from the jackdaw's chest.

"Mine! Mine! Mine!" cheeped and squawked the other birds, plucking their feathers out. Ashamed and bedraggled, the poor jackdaw promised, "I'll never put on borrowed finery again."

Birds were highly respected in ancient times. Goddess Hera's favorite bird was a peacock.

The Hare *and* The Tortoise

"TORTOISE, you're such a slowpoke," said Hare. "Me, I'm really fast."

Tortoise replied, "I get to where I'm going in my own good time." And she challenged Hare to a race.

"A race? Against *me*?" Hare laughed and laughed. "All right. I'll race you down to that willow tree. Ready, get set, go!"

He sprinted forward, lightning fast.

Tortoise set off at her pace.

In a jiffy Hare was more than half the way there. "I'll take a little nap," he thought, and stretched out in the sun.

He slept while Tortoise lumbered along.

On she lumbered, slow and steady . . .

When Hare awoke, Tortoise had nearly reached the willow.

Hare jumped up and ran and ran and ran . . . but too late. Tortoise won!

Aesop's master Iadmon, also owned Rhodopis, a very beautiful young woman-slave. Maybe she and Aesop worked side by side and were good friends.

The Eagle *and* The Fighting Cocks

"I AM king of the farmyard," a golden cock crowed.

A paler cock challenged, "Says who?"

Soon feathers flew in all directions as these two enemies hacked at each other with sharp beaks and claws.

The paler cock proved stronger. He forced the other into a corner, then flew up onto a wall. "I won! I'm king of the farmyard," he loudly let the whole world know.

Maybe a little *too* loudly.

A hungry eagle heard him and came plummeting down . . .

The golden cock, defeated, cowered in the corner and watched the eagle snatch the winner away.

Then he, the loser, flew up onto that same wall and crowed, "Guess who's king of the farmyard now?"

The 6th-century poet Sappho lived on the island of Lesbos, not far from Samos. It's possible that she knew Aesop. Many of her poems are still read today.

The Shepherd Boy *and* The Wolf

 "**A**LL the sheep ever do is say 'baa' and munch grass," thought the shepherd boy. He wished something would happen.

"I know: I'll invent some excitement."

He cupped his hands to his mouth and shouted: "Help, a wolf is near!"

The villagers came running. "Where's the wolf?" they asked.

The shepherd boy laughed and said, "Fooled you!"

Another day, for fun, he cried, "Wolf! Wolf!" again. The villagers came running — and were fooled again.

One day a wolf really did appear, hungrily eyeing the sheep. "Help! WOLF!" the shepherd boy yelled, terrified. "This time it's really true!"

But nobody believed him.

Well, *you* know what happened: The wolf killed many sheep that day and had himself a mutton feast. The shepherd boy was sorry and never cried "wolf" again.

No one knows what Aesop looked like. But people like to think that he was short and misshapen. An ungainly figure, but with a brilliant mind.

The Tortoise *and* The Eagle

ORTOISE gazed up and saw birds gliding about in the sky. They looked so free and feathery. "I wish that I could fly," she complained. "Oh, how I envy them!"

Tortoise sighed, then cried aloud, "Won't somebody please teach me to fly? I'd give anything if only I knew how!"

"Get ready, then," somebody screeched. It was Eagle.

He came swooping down.

He grasped Tortoise in his talons. Up he soared, past mountain peaks and higher.

Tortoise was thrilled. "But when can I fly on my own?" she asked.

"Now!" Eagle replied, and suddenly let go.

But instead of flying, Tortoise crashed down, heavy as a stone, and was smashed to bits.

Socrates, the great philosopher, was put in jail for staying true to his beliefs. Legend has it that he whiled away his prison days by putting Aesop's fables into verse.

The Monkey and The Dolphin

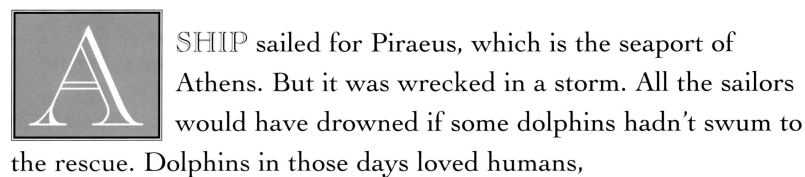

A SHIP sailed for Piraeus, which is the seaport of Athens. But it was wrecked in a storm. All the sailors would have drowned if some dolphins hadn't swum to the rescue. Dolphins in those days loved humans, especially Athenians.

One sailor on the ship had his pet monkey with him.
Mistaking the monkey for a man, a dolphin invited him,
"Climb on my back. You are Athenian, aren't you?"

"I am indeed," the monkey answered.

"Then you must know Piraeus," said the dolphin.

"Yes, I know him well," bragged the monkey, thinking that
Piraeus was a famous citizen of Athens.

The dolphin laughed. Yes, animals could laugh back then.
He shook the silly monkey off and plunged into the waves.

The ancient Greeks were great seafarers with far-reaching trade routes. Piraeus was Athens' seaport in ancient times and still is to this day.

The Wolf and The Crane

OLF gulped down a big chunk of meat — much too fast. He gasped and nearly choked. A bone was stuck in his throat.

What was he going to do?

He spied a crane nearby.

"Crane, Crane," he croaked, "come and help me, and I'll pay you well!"

Crane came over from the swamp. Skillfully using his long, thin beak, he dislodged the bone and pulled it out.

"There, it's done. Now, Wolf, how will you pay me?" he asked.

"I've paid you already," Wolf said, grinning, and flashed his sharp, big teeth.

"How so?" asked Crane.

"You stuck your head in a wolf's mouth, and didn't get bitten.

"Is that not payment enough?"

In medieval times, before there were printed books, Aesop's fables were pictured on dishes, in handlettered books, and on cloth.

The Lion *and* The Man

ION and Man went walking through the woods together.

"I'm stronger. I have sharper teeth. I eat my victims raw," bragged Lion.

"Well, I'm smarter. I have weapons and fire. I cook my food, it's tastier that way," said Man.

"I don't care, I'm better," Lion claimed.

"No, I am," boasted Man.

They came to a clearing and saw a statue. It was of a man defeating a lion in battle.

"You see?" said Man. "This statue proves that I'm the better of us two."

"But think," said Lion, smiling. "If a *lion* had sculpted the statue, who do you suppose the conqueror would be?"

Ancient Greek sculptors (all men, no lions) created many splendid statues, such as this one of Aphrodite of Knidos by Praxiteles.

Aesop